UP THE MOUNTAIN

STORY AND PICTURES BY

Charlotte Agell

DORLING KINDERSLEY PUBLISHING, INC.

For Anders Torsten Christopher Höckert,
his family and mine!

A Richard Jackson Book

Dorling Kindersley Publishing, Inc., 95 Madison Avenue, New York, New York 10016
Visit us on the World Wide Web at http://www.dk.com

Dorling Kindersley books are available at special discounts for bulk purchases for sales promotions or premiums. Special editions, including
personalized covers, excerpts of existing guides, and corporate imprints can be created in large quantities for specific needs. For more informa-
tion, contact Special Markets Dept., Dorling Kindersley Publishing, Inc., 95 Madison Avenue, New York, New York 10016; fax (800) 600-9098.

Library of Congress Cataloging-in-Publication Data
Agell, Charlotte.
Up the mountain / story and pictures by Charlotte Agell. — 1st ed.
p. cm.
Summary: Cat, Rabbit, Chicken, and Dragon go for a rainy romp up the mountain,
splashing in puddles until the moon beckons them back home.
ISBN 0-7894-2610-2   [1. Mountains—Fiction. 2. Rain and rainfall—Fiction. 3. Animals—Fiction. 4. Stories in rhyme.]
I. Title. PZ8.3.A2595Up 2000 [E]—dc21 98-44863 CIP AC

Book design by Jennifer Browne. The illustrations for this book were created with watercolor, India ink, and oil pastels.
The text of this book is set in 32 point Cheltenham Light. Printed and bound in U.S.A.

First Edition, 2000
2 4 6 8 10 9 7 5 3 1

Morning

Rain...

Cloudy day.

Let's go walking
anyway!

Two umbrellas.
We can share.

Puddles!
Splashes everywhere.

Red rain boots
and muddy feet

Dancing wetly
down the street.

Up the mountain?
In the rain?

We can always go
back home again.....

Climbing up
the rocky path

Dragon takes
a sudden bath!

Cat and Rabbit
run ahead.

Chicken stops
to rest instead.

Cold and hungry
in the rain—

We can always go
back home again!

Still—the top is near,
the trees are fewer.

Magically,
the sky is bluer!

An umbrella
makes a walking stick.

And there are
blackberries to pick.

Above the world
we sit and dream—

The wind, a leaf,
a little stream . . .

How far away
the distance seems.

The sun is sinking.
Shadows grow.

It's getting late,
it's time to go....

Down the mountain.
Look! The moon!

Mosquitoes hum
a biting tune.

Day or night,
in moon or rain,

it's good to be
back home again.

Night!